# SOUNDS LIKE FUN

By J.L. Anderson

Illustrated by Alan Brown

Rourke
Educational Media
rourkeeducationalmedia.com

www.rourkeeducationalmedia.com

Edited by: Keli Sipperley
Cover and Interior layout by: Rhea Magaro-Wallace
Cover and Interior Illustrations by: Alan Brown

## Library of Congress PCN Data

Sounds Like Fun / J.L. Anderson
(Paisley Atoms)
ISBN (hard cover)(alk. paper) 978-1-68191-718-4
ISBN (soft cover) 978-1-68191-819-8
ISBN (e-Book) 978-1-68191-914-0
Library of Congress Control Number: 2016932596

Printed in the United States of America,
North Mankato, Minnesota

*Dear Parents and Teachers,*

*Future world-famous scientist Paisley Atoms and her best friend, Ben Striker, aren't afraid to stir things up in their quests for discovery. Using Paisley's basement as a laboratory, the two are constantly inventing, exploring, and, well, making messes. Paisley has a few bruises to show for their work, too. She wears them like badges of honor.*

*These fast-paced adventures weave fascinating facts, quotes from real scientists, and explanations for various phenomena into witty dialogue, stealthily boosting your reader's understanding of multiple science topics. From sound waves to dinosaurs, from the sea floor to the moon, Paisley, Ben and the gang are perfect partner resources for a STEAM curriculum.*

*Each illustrated chapter book includes a science experiment or activity, a biography of a woman in science, jokes, and websites to visit.*

*In addition, each book also includes online teacher/parent notes with ideas for incorporating the story into a lesson plan. These notes include subject matter, background information, inspiration for maker space activities, comprehension questions, and additional online resources. Notes are available at: www.RourkeEducationalMedia.com.*

*We hope you enjoy Paisley and her pals as much as we do.*

*Happy reading,*
*Rourke Educational Media*

# TABLE OF CONTENTS

# CHAPTER ONE
# MUSIC HALL MYSTERY

Paisley Atoms rolled up her pants to show off the scab on her shin. Some girls at school like Whitney-Raelynn said scabs were "icky-sicky," but Paisley saw them as a badge of honor. She sort of hoped it would leave a cool scar, at least for a little while.

"Ahem," Whitney-Raelynn said, staring at Paisley. She pointed at the scab and pretended to gag dramatically. If she wanted a reaction, Paisley wasn't biting. She just flashed a friendly smile. She also smiled at Mrs. Decibel as she waltzed into the music room, her long dress swishing and her charm bracelet clanging.

Mrs. Decibel once won an award for Best Dressed at Roarington Elementary. Today's dress was especially award-winning. Rosalind swiveled her wheelchair to get a better look at the embroidered musical notes on the puffy dress.

Paisley noted that while Mrs. Decibel dressed elegantly, her hair and her facial expression didn't quite match. The music teacher's hair was up in a bun, and it was messy like Paisley's, only unlike Paisley's, it usually didn't look that way.

Suki raised her hand, and before Mrs. Decibel could call on her, she blurted out, "What's the deal with your outfit?"

"Yeah, are you about to get married to a conductor or something?" Arjun asked.

"I'm already married. My MaestraSingers group is about to perform with the orchestra, but I'm not sure it will be so special." Mrs. Decibel tugged at her bun and frowned. "Will you please move that xylophone off of the risers, Suki?" she added.

"I'm Sumi."

Mrs. Decibel glanced at Suki and then at her identical twin sister Sumi. They were hard to tell apart. Ben could get it right most of the time, but Paisley was correct at identifying them a hundred percent of the time.

"Sorry to confuse you two," Mrs. Decibel said.

"I'm actually Sumi," the real Sumi said with a grin.

"I just can't help myself." Suki giggled as she moved the xylophone out of the way. She clanged one of the keys loudly by accident.

Arjun held his hands over his ears. "Ow! My ears are ringing now. I think you fractured my stapes!" he said. Paisley and Ben both knew the stapes was the bone in the middle of the ears of humans and mammals that conducts the sound vibrations to the inner ear. It paid off that Paisley's dad was a biologist.

Normally, Mrs. Decibel would've laughed at the students' antics, but she just pulled a few more strands of hair out of her bun.

"Okay, okay. Let's begin our exercises for today," Mrs. Decibel said.

"Time to exercise!" Rosalind yelled. She pumped her arms in the air before clapping. She wheeled in front of the risers then spun around in a circle on only one wheel of her wheelchair.

The entire class broke into a mixture of laughter and applause.

Mrs. Decibel's hair was lopsided now. Her lips quivered and her eyes filled with tears. It was rare to see a teacher cry at Roarington Elementary, and if it did happen, it was usually just Mrs. Decibel's eyes watering from laughing so hard. Their music teacher was a gifted singer and even had a musical laugh. At this moment, she was completely silent.

"Uh oh, something is really wrong," Paisley whispered to Ben.

Ben nodded. Paisley had been friends with him so long that she could tell that he was worried about their teacher too just by the way he moved his head.

Rosalind pulled off another spectacular trick in her wheelchair, but Paisley didn't have time to be impressed. She moved forward to give Mrs. Decibel

a hug. Paisley's mom seemed to think a hug was an answer for everything. Most of the time, it did help, even if just a teensy fraction of a little bit.

The class quieted down and Whitney-Raelynn elbowed Ben out of the way to hug Mrs. Decibel next. After more hugs and a few apologies, Mrs. Decibel wiped her eyes.

"Can you tell us what's wrong?" Ben asked.

Mrs. Decibel sat down on the risers with her students. "The MaestraSingers have been working so hard. We're a talented group of singers, you know, but the new music hall makes us sound horrid. Tonight is our dress rehearsal before the grand opening celebration tomorrow and we'll be the joke of Roarington." She began to tear up again and the class fussed over her.

"Oh, you all are the sweetest students ever. I'll be okay. It's just a silly concert anyway. Now let's get to exer—" Mrs. Decibel started say "exercise" again but caught herself. "Let's begin making some music."

Science class followed music, but as much as Paisley loved science, she wasn't in her usual rush.

"We have to find a way to help Mrs. Decibel," Paisley whispered to Ben.

"Paisley Atoms late for science class?" Ben asked, glancing at the wristwatch he'd made. He was named after Benjamin Banneker, a famous scientist, astronomer, and clockmaker. Funny enough, Ben liked all those things too.

"There's a first for everything," Paisley said, then winked. "Maybe the time on your watch isn't right."

"Doubtful," Ben said. Like Benjamin Banneker, he'd taken a watch apart to study and then made his own using wooden parts he fashioned like the original. Unlike Benjamin Banneker, Ben never could get the original watch fully back together again, though to his credit, it did keep correct time.

Paisley and Ben approached Mrs. Decibel. She tinkered with her charm bracelet.

"We'd like to help you solve the sound problem," Ben said.

"Oh, thank you! There isn't much time before the concert and the MaestraSingers could use all the help we can get," Mrs. Decibel said. She gave them the directions to the new music hall and said she'd meet them later at the dress rehearsal as long as they got permission from their parents.

"I bet you two will be closing the instrument case soon," Dad said when Paisley called him. She could hear her rescued pet mongoose, Newton, chattering in the background.

Paisley had high hopes he was right. She and Ben wanted to make Mrs. Decibel's high notes sound as good as possible.

# CHAPTER TWO
# SOUND ISSUES

"Where are you two going?" Whitney-Raelynn asked Ben and Paisley as they quickly packed up their backpacks at the end of the school day.

Paisley was about to tell Whitney-Raelynn that she should mind her own business when Ben said, "We plan on solving the music hall sound mystery."

"If I didn't have such an important afterschool project, I'd go fix the sound system myself," Whitney-Raelynn said. She paused for a moment as if she expected them to ask about her plans.

When Paisley and Ben stayed silent, she explained anyway. "I'm taking voice lessons to learn how to project my voice even better than I already do. I'm going to win the spelling bee no matter what, but confidence is key!" she said, and then chuckled at her own comment. "Punny-funny, get it? Key as in matching a note to a scale?"

"Prepare to get pitched," Paisley said under her breath.

"I'm sure you'll do great," Ben said.

Whitney-Raelynn stood a little taller as she waved goodbye and walked off.

"Why would you feed her ego like that?" Paisley asked Ben when she was out of earshot.

"I wanted to hurry up and get to the music hall. Besides, she tends to be great at almost everything whether we like it or not," Ben said.

Paisley couldn't argue with that, but their conversation with her rival had given her an idea. "Do you think the singers aren't projecting their voices loud enough?"

"The MaestraSingers and the orchestra have had a lot of practice and I don't think they lack confidence at all," Ben said.

Again, he was right. Paisley thought about all of the trophies and pictures of Mrs. Decibel singing as the lead in various concerts.

"There could be something wrong with the building or the microphones," Paisley said.

"Or the instruments could be placed in the wrong area and it could drown out the singers' voices," Ben said.

These were all good ideas, but it didn't narrow the problem down very much. They would have to spend time exploring the equipment, the instruments, and the entire building with not much time remaining before the grand opening performance.

The walk to the music hall was a long one, but Paisley and Ben kept things interesting by practicing for the spelling bee, too. Sure, Whitney-Raelynn was known as Grammar Girl, but Paisley and Ben were good at lots of stuff besides science and math.

Paisley focused on spelling words related to sound as she quizzed Ben. "Acoustics. The study of sound and sound waves. We're going to figure out what is wrong with the acoustics—"

Ben replied before Paisley could finish the sentence. "Acoustics. A-c-o-u-s-t-i-c-s. Acoustics."

"You can't interrupt the judge, Ben, or you'll never win," Paisley said.

"Okay, okay. Let me think of a good one for you," Ben said.

When they got to downtown Roarington, or Boring Town as Paisley called it, they passed a worker breaking up concete at the construction site of a new dental office. That new addition to their quiet town wasn't nearly as exciting or as entertaining as a new music hall.

"I thought of a good one!" Ben finally said. "Frequency. The number of times something is repeated in a period of time. Hertz is the unit used to measure the frequency of sound waves. Frequency."

Paisley took a deep breath. "Frequency. F-r-e-q-" She paused, then said, "If we could somehow turn into sound waves, we could solve the mystery much quicker."

"True, but you can't get distracted like that or you'll lose the spelling bee."

Whitney-Raelynn definitely had the advantage there. Paisley got distracted a lot.

Paisley started over, which technically wasn't against spelling bee rules as long as she didn't get the letters out of order. "Frequency. F-r-e-q-u-e-n-c-y. Frequency."

Ben clapped for her. They gave the spelling bee practice a break as soon as they got to the Music Hall of Roarington. The name might've been bland, but the bright red brick building was modern and exciting. It was much taller than the office buildings that surrounded it, though not nearly as tall as the nearby water tower. The display had flashing lights and played a loud melody. The sign read, "Grand Opening Tomorrow!"

"Is it just me or is that sign crooked?" Paisley asked,

tilting her head to get a better look.

"I didn't notice how crooked it is right away," Ben said.

"I wonder why it's like that?" Paisley answered her own question with another question. "Maybe as a way of catching your attention so you'll read the sign?"

"That's probably the only explanation that makes sense," Ben said, waving at Mrs. Decibel, who came over to greet them.

Her bun seemed even more severe than before. It gave Paisley a headache just thinking about her own messy bun being bound that tightly.

"I'm so glad you are here. I think the sound is even worse today," Mrs. Decibel said as she led them into the music hall.

The building smelled like new lumber. The stage was enormous, with plenty of seats for the audience. A skylight in the ceiling made the hall bright and cheerful.

A huge, regal purple drape hung against the back wall. Paisley thought something like that would look good in her house. The purple would make all of her mom's and dad's botanical and biological specimens stand out. Ben had his eyes on the wrought iron clock on the side wall.

Mrs. Decibel introduced Paisley and Ben to the MaestraSingers. They were all just as decked out and stressed out as the music teacher.

Paisley and Ben sat in the box seats to listen to the rehearsal to get a better sense of what was going on. Mrs. Decibel hadn't exaggerated about how terrible things sounded.

A drummer drummed, but it sounded more like a tapping noise. The singers seemed to be singing their hearts out, but it was hard to hear them.

Paisley and Ben moved to the back of the hall to see if changing location helped, but it made the sound even worse. If Paisley and Ben couldn't fix things, the attendees were all going to ask for a refund and the music hall might close soon after opening.

Paisley leaned into to Ben to whisper, "No wonder why Mrs. Decibel broke down in class today."

At that moment, something sounded long and low, much like a train whistle. It didn't seem to be coming from any of the orchestra members on the stage or from any of the singers.

"What did you say?" Ben asked.

"The music sounds weak and distorted. No wonder Mrs. Decibel started crying," Paisley said. If Paisley had worked this hard and been as excited about the grand opening, she might've been crying, too.

"We should interview the building engineer," Ben said. He took a moment to draw a diagram of the music hall in his field journal. He took a few extra moments to draw the clock and even did a little sketch of what he imagined the gears to look like inside.

"I also have another idea," Paisley said, bouncing on her toes.

"Oh man, I have a feeling things are about to get… interesting," Ben said.

# CHAPTER THREE
# TRANSFORMATION!

Paisley and Ben wandered onto the stage. It was really thrilling to be in the middle of all of the instruments looking out into the audience. Paisley wondered if maybe she should take some kind of music, acting, or voice projecting classes. If she did, she decided she would keep it a secret, unlike someone else she knew.

A sound like a jackhammer smashing concrete filled the air.

"We should cancel the performance," one of the MaestraSingers, Ms. Gossett, said to Mrs. Decibel.

Mrs. Decibel sighed. "It might be best to reschedule."

"You all sounded really good…when we were right next to you," Paisley said.

"Oh dear. There's no way we can fit the entire audience on the stage. People will be driving in from all parts of the state," Mrs. Decibel said. "Have you two figured anything out?"

Paisley didn't want to let her teacher down. "We… uh, we've got a few clues."

"Can we speak to the building engineer?" Ben asked.

Ms. Gossett shook her head. "Several of us have tried to talk to him to find out what's wrong with this place, but there is a rumor he's been fired."

There went that lead to find out more information.

"Feel free to explore while we get some refreshments," Mrs. Decibel said.

Ben's eyes flew back to the clock. Paisley went right for the drum set. She beat the drum sticks against the drum. The vibrations moved all the way up her arms.

Ben hummed into the microphone. "Seems to be projecting at this range," he said. Ben tinkered with a few more instruments and strummed on a guitar.

"Can you imagine us in a rock band some day?" Paisley asked.

Ben smiled. Just like his nod, the smile said it all.

"So about my idea," Paisley said. She held up the drum stick. "I really think we could devise something to turn us into sound waves. We could interact with the environment for clues."

The two of them had shared many exciting scientific adventures together, but turning into sound waves to solve a mystery? That would be a first.

Paisley held up the drum stick and wondered how she could make it vibrate to create a pressure wave. It was made of wood. Something metal would do a better job creating vibrations to send them into the air. If they could make it work, of course.

"Do you think we could find a tuning fork?" Paisley asked. She shuffled around the orchestra equipment looking for a rod with a U-shaped fork that makes a certain pitch. No luck.

"I want to try something," Ben said. He found a folding ladder behind the stage and moved it over to the clock he'd been admiring.

"Really, Ben? I know how much you like clocks and all, but we don't have time to waste. The performers will be back from break any moment and time is ticking."

"Good pun, Paisley, but think like a proton and stay positive," Ben said.

Ben was taller than Paisley, but she was a better climber so she volunteered to get the clock without understanding why.

She normally didn't get dizzy, but the lights in the building were bright and the clock seemed extra high as she climbed.

Paisley gasped. The ladder swayed as she reached for the clock. She'd forgotten to check to make sure the ladder was properly secured.

"Careful!" Ben said.

"You better be worried about me and not the clock," Paisley called down. She thought she could hear Ben chuckle.

The large clock filled her arms, which made getting down even more challenging. She missed a step.

Paisley lost her grasp on the clock. "Oh no!"

Paisley clung to the side of the ladder until she could safely plant her feet on the rung. The clock, though? She had to let it go. "Watch out, Ben!"

Ben caught the clock flying in the air with such grace, Paisley thought he looked like a circus performer. He set the clock down and helped Paisley off the ladder.

"Watch out? You're out-punning Whitney-Raelynn," Ben said.

Paisley laughed. "Too bad Whitney-Raelynn didn't hear my spectacular punny funny. Then again, she would've also seen me nearly fall off a ladder."

"She also missed stellar clock catch!" Ben added.

Paisley groaned and rolled her eyes. "Fill me in about the clock already. I practically risked our lives for it."

Ben pointed to the second hand of the clock. "See how it makes a tick-tock motion as it moves to each second? This means it is a quartz watch instead of mechanical one. Inside the clock, there is a tiny quartz—"

"Tuning fork!" Paisley guessed.

"Well, let's hope I'm not wrong," Ben said. He took the clock apart without needing anything other than the small tool set he always kept in his pocket.

"Ben, you're a genius!" Paisley said when he pulled out a quartz crystal resonator in the shape of a tuning fork.

Paisley heard some chatter in the distance, though the sound in the music hall wasn't reliable. Dress rehearsal break must've ended. "We have to hurry!"

Paisley pulled out the ancient key she wore around her neck and pressed it against the tiny quartz tuning fork. "Please let us become sound waves," she requested.

She bumped her fist against Ben's and they chanted, "Science Alliance!"

The tiny quartz tuning fork began to vibrate. She set it down on Mrs. Decibel's music stand to let it do its thing.

Paisley couldn't hear anything. "Do you think it is working?"

"This vibrates in the ultrasonic range," Ben said.

A moment later, Paisley felt pressure all over her skin.

Then, they transformed into sound waves! Paisley hadn't felt this lightweight since traveling to outer space.

"This is cool," Paisley tried to say, though it was more like a thought floating in the air that only Ben could understand.

As sound waves, they were energy about to make a journey.

# CHAPTER FOUR
# INTERFERENCE

The vibrations from the tiny tuning fork pulled and pushed them in the air. They didn't get too far, though.

Ben clashed against the wrought iron frame of the clock. "Ouch!"

Paisley tried to keep the same thing from happening to her, but the force bounced her right into the clock, too. "Owie." If she didn't know better, she might've thought the clock was trying to get back at her for almost dropping it.

Ben was about to hit another part of the clock when Paisley pushed through the air to steer him away.

"Thanks, Paisley," Ben said. "The clock might be amazing, but it sure did hurt."

"No kidding!" If Paisley were in her human form, she would've rubbed her head. "If sound reacts that way to the metal parts of the clock, why would it be in a music hall?"

"I was just thinking the same thing. A different clock should be in here, one that doesn't create interference. This one has to go," Ben said.

As soon as the word "go" was out of his mouth, Paisley and Ben danced through the air once again.

This time, they bumped on the metal chairs in the auditorium. Ben clanged against a bolt securing the chair to the ground. "The metal is reflecting sounds," he said.

"Ouch!" they called out together in perfect harmony. Paisley hit a metal bar at the top of the chair and reflected off of it with force.

"That's going to leave a bruise," Paisley said.

Just like scars, she didn't mind bruises. The exception was a black eye because then her mom would make a big deal out of it. Mom might never let Paisley forget about the time she got a black eye right before her fifth grade school pictures.

"Funny that I didn't notice all this metal on the chairs when we were checking things out earlier," Ben said.

"Me neither," Paisley said. She glanced around to see just how many chairs there were in the audience.

"Several hundred," Ben said as if he had a similar thought.

"That's a whole lot of sound interference," Paisley said.

Just like the clock, these chairs had to go to improve the sound in the building.

"Uh oh," Paisley said as she was pulled to more pieces of metal in the new music hall. She hit her head against a doorknob.

"Is it possible for sound waves to get a concussion?" Paisley asked.

Ben crashed into the door hinge and a few door knobs. "If we continue at this rate, we just might."

A lock gave Paisley a lump. "Ouch. Ouch! OUCH!"

"Seriously, why is there so much metal everywhere? Didn't the engineer realize that it would create unwanted vibrations? This is a really painful way to find out answers," Ben said.

"It could explain why the building engineer might've gotten fired," Paisley said as she kept getting painfully bounced around.

Paisley hadn't thought about this part of the adventure.

Moments later, they were sucked up by something huge and purple. The curtain!

At least the fabric slowed them down and comfortably caught them up in its plush fibers. It was nice to take a break from all the crashing around.

"I could stay here all day to recover," Paisley said.

"Me too," Ben replied. "That's an issue, though. Sound shouldn't be getting trapped in a curtain like this."

"Good point," Paisley said "Unlike the metal that reflected us, the soft fibers absorbed us."

Her energy lowered as she struggled to get out of the curtain.

"The fibers are gathering me in and won't let me go," Ben said.

"It's not time for a nap," Paisley said, "and you should never sleep if you might have a concussion."

With her help, Ben broke free and they both bounced off the wooden wall in the back of the room.

"Whee! That's fun," Paisley said, wanting to bounce again.

"The building is supposed to freely reflect energy like this," Ben said.

"Then why is the purple curtain here?" Paisley asked. "Do you think someone put it here on accident or purpose?"

"I don't know," Ben said, bouncing off of another wooden surface.

When would Paisley have an opportunity to do this again? She pinged against the wood and felt full of energy and excitement.

The wooden surfaces were fun to bounce against, unlike the metal pieces. There were a few other smaller drapes that Paisley and Ben tried to avoid getting sucked into again.

When Paisley pinged off a column, she felt herself lifting high in the air.

"Wait for me!" Ben called.

Paisley couldn't control where she was going. She sailed up toward the roof of the building. It felt like a roller coaster ride as she was sucked up closer and closer to the skylight.

"Bad news!" Ben said.

Paisley understood a moment later what he was worried about. The skylight didn't have a seal around it to keep the outside air, weather, and noise out of the building.

They were being sucked up and out of the building. Roarington might not have been the most exciting of towns, but there were all kinds of things happening outside that Paisley and Ben might interact with as

sound waves. They could easily get hurt.

They moved at an even swifter pace as they headed right toward the dental building construction site.

The jackhammer might do something even worse than give them a concussion.

# CHAPTER FIVE
# ADVENTURE
# AND ANSWERS

"Where's the tuning fork?" Ben asked.

Paisley remembered she'd set it down back in the building. That wouldn't do them any good.

"I'm done being a sound wave!" Paisley called out. She tried to reach for her necklace, but in her current state, that was impossible.

Nothing happened.

The jackhammer attacked the ground again. A cloud of concrete dust rose up. Paisley could only imagine how much this was going to hurt.

Ben spewed out some number about how many seconds it would be until they were destroyed. Paisley had to ignore him so she would stay calm.

"I'm done being a sound wave!" Paisley repeated, just in case it might work the second time around.

They were still flying forward.

Then something changed their course.

Lights started flashing on the display and the loud melody boomed. "Grand Opening Tomorrow!"

Paisley spun around in the air. The construction worker stopped using the jackhammer and stared in their direction.

"Wow, that was a close call," Paisley said. She no longer felt lightweight. No wonder why the construction worker kept staring at them. They'd shifted back into their human forms right before his eyes.

Paisley brought her hand to her throat. "I'm so glad we're okay," she said, feeling her vocal cords vibrate against her fingers. There was so much about sound she took for granted every day.

"That was quite an adventure," Ben said. He brought his hands to his throat for the same reason and then he checked out some of his bruises.

Paisley would have some colorful ones on her arms. She wanted to wear a tank top to show them off. Grammar Girl would surely have some comment to make about that, but Paisley was too proud to care. They'd made some important discoveries.

Paisley and Ben recapped everything they'd learned during their time as sound waves. There were too many pieces of metal in the building between the clock, the locks, and the chairs. This made the acoustics sound off by the way the sound reflected. It made sounds louder, and it made them echo.

The huge purple drape and the other fabrics absorbed sounds. The skylight needed to have a good seal. No wonder they could hear the train in the distance, as well as the jackhammer. Sound could not only get in, it could also escape.

They walked back into the music hall and spotted Mrs. Decibel. They needed to share what they'd learned. Perhaps these problems could be fixed in time for the grand opening.

Before they could say anything, Mrs. Decibel held up the tuning fork. "Have you ever seen such a tiny one?" She shook it for good measure.

Paisley flinched like she was about to turn into a sound wave again.

"I can't figure how this must've gotten on my music stand. It will look really cute on my charm bracelet," Mrs. Decibel said.

Paisley and Ben grinned at each other. Hopefully the tuning fork would lose its power so they would stay in their human forms from here on out. Unless, of course, the need arose to transform again. *You never know*, Paisley thought.

Some of the orchestra players started practicing again, so Paisley raised her voice to explain what she and Ben discovered.

"How in the world did we not notice these things?"

Ms. Gossett exclaimed.

Several of the other MaestraSingers moved closer to listen in as Paisley and Ben shared their suspicions.

"I think someone might've sabotaged the acoustics," Paisley said. "There are too many things out of place. It seems like it was done on purpose rather than an accident. Even the display outside is crooked."

She didn't want to jump to any conclusion, but the other singers came up with all sorts of ideas as the dress rehearsal wrapped up for the day.

"The building engineer probably didn't know what he was doing," one of them said.

"Maybe he did know what he was doing, but made all of these changes after he got fired," another said.

"Thanks, Paisley and Ben. I plan to make several phone calls to get this sorted out," Mrs. Decibel said. "It is good to know the mayor and the police chief at a time like this. We at least know why things sound terrible in the building, but now we have to fix them in time for tomorrow. I guess we'll all have to stay tuned."

Paisley's pet mongoose, Newton, ran up her leg as soon as she got home. After a mongoose cuddle session, Dad took Paisley and Ben out to eat at El Rancho, where there was a lively group of mariachi singers. There definitely was nothing wrong with the acoustics in the restaurant.

"Things will work out, you'll see," Dad reassured them. "You guys made some important discoveries."

Mom said the same thing when Paisley video chatted with her later that evening. "Hola, *mija*," Mom said. She had a pink and white dahlia pushed behind her ear, the national flower of Mexico.

"Hi, Mom!"

"Where'd you get that bruise on your shoulder?" Mom asked. Mom never missed anything, even if she was currently in Mexico studying plants.

Paisley filled her in on their sound wave adventure.

"You and Ben are so smart. The hardest part after making a big discovery is waiting to see what is going to happen next," Mom said.

The wait felt especially long. The next day, Mrs. Decibel told Paisley and Ben that the building engineer had indeed sabotaged the acoustics in the new music hall.

He'd missed too many days of work, so the construction company fired him. To get back at the company, he fixed metal hardware to the seats and the doors, plus added the drapes. He also never finished the skylight.

"He worked out a deal with the mayor and the police chief and brought in a work crew to fix the problems before the grand opening tonight," Mrs. Decibel said. "As part of his deal, he'll be paying for a lot of the community to go free of charge, including all of Roarington Elementary."

The whole school couldn't stop talking about the grand opening celebration. All the kids kept stopping Paisley and Ben in the hallway to say thanks. Well, except for Whitney-Raelynn. She wouldn't be able to go because she had her voice projection lessons.

Paisley knew she needed to be practicing for the

upcoming spelling bee, but for now, she wanted to enjoy the evening's celebration.

Dad even dressed up for the event. He wore a tie with acoustic waves on it.

Arjun wore a suit. Suki and Sumi wore different dresses so everyone could tell them apart. Rosalind made herself a rose crown that matched her dress. She also decorated her wheelchair with a few roses.

Paisley and Ben looked over the entire building and confirmed that the building engineer made all needed changes. The only thing that wasn't fixed was the display. It stayed just as crooked. Turns out the mayor liked it better that way because it really was more eye-catching.

"You can have the clock," Mrs. Decibel said to Ben. "It isn't working anymore and we all know you can fix it."

Paisley looked at the tiny tuning fork on Mrs. Decibel's charm bracelet and tried not to giggle.

"Instrument case closed," Paisley said, high-fiving Ben.

# Science Alliance!
# Make Your Own Kazoo

You can experiment with sound by making your own kazoo. Your voice will travel down the tube to the wax paper attached on the end. The wax paper will then vibrate and change the way your voice sounds.

## Materials
- toilet paper roll or any cardboard tube
- wax paper
- rubber band
- scissors

### Step 1

Hold the wax paper over the tube and measure out a piece that is over an inch (2.54 centimeters) larger than the opening of the cardboard tube.

### Step 2

Wrap the wax paper over one end of the tube. Hold it in place with the rubber band.

### Step 3

Put the open end of the kazoo up to your mouth and hum, sing, whisper, or shout into it to see how it makes your voice sound different.

## Women in Science

Scientist Emeritus Elizabeth T. Bunce (1915–2003) was the first American woman to serve as chief scientist on a major oceanographic expedition. Her many research interests included underwater acoustics, or the study of how sound travels underwater. The Bunce Fault, the deepest part of the Atlantic Ocean, was named in her honor.

## Author Q & A

**Q: Any surprises while researching the book?**
A: I had no idea how much work went into perfecting the acoustics at a concert hall!

**Q: If you could turn into a sound wave, where would you go?**
A: I think it would be fascinating to experience ocean sounds.

**Q: Who is one of your favorite characters to write about?**
A: I love Paisley and Ben, of course, but Whitney-Raelynn has been such a fun character to develop.

## Silly Science!

Q: **What did the receiver say when the radio wave injured it?**

A: Hey, that megahertz!

Q: **What did the dog say to his owner?**

A: "My favorite frequency is 50,000 hertz but you've probably never heard that."

## Websites to Visit

**To learn more about concert hall acoustics:**

*www.acoustics.salford.ac.uk/acoustics_info/
 concert_hall_acoustics/?content=index*

**For some interesting facts about sound:**

*www.sciencekids.co.nz/sciencefacts/sound.html*

**Facts and concepts related to sound:**

*www.buzzle.com/articles/
 sound-waves-for-kids.html*

## About the Author

J.L. Anderson's education inspired her to become an author, but she thought seriously about becoming a biologist, and she once was the president of the science club in high school. She lives outside of Austin, Texas with her husband, daughter, and two naughty dogs. You can learn more about her at www.jessicaleeanderson.com.

## About the Illustrator

Alan Brown's love of comic art, cartoons and drawing has driven him to follow his dreams of becoming an artist. His career as a freelance artist and designer has allowed him to work on a wide range of projects, from magazine illustration and game design to children's books. He's had the good fortune to work on comics such as *Ben 10* and *Bravest Warriors*. Alan lives in Newcastle with his wife, sons and dog.